DOTTY

THE LADY!
...PLAYS HIDE-

Illustrated by Jon

a **Joshua Morris** book
from **The Reader's Digest Association, Inc.**

Dotty loves playing hide-and-seek.
You can help her if you peek.

Who's hiding there behind the thicket?
Yes, you're right. It's . . .

In that flower – can you see?

Look who's hiding. It's . . .

Guess who's hiding near the plant?

I can guess. It's . . .

Who's that hiding by the lake?

Look who's there. It's . . .

Who thinks her web will surely hide her?

Peek-a-boo! It's . . .

Who's hiding in the bush nearby?

It's . . .

Be very quiet, and please don't squirm,

Or Dotty will find you . . .

It's fun to search both far and wide.
Let's play again. Who wants to hide?